095497

Farris, Pamela J.
  Young mouse and elephant.

**Colusa County Free Library**

**738 Market Street**
**Colusa, CA   95932**
**Phone : 458-7671**

# Young Mouse and Elephant

*An East African Folktale*

Adapted by **Pamela J. Farris**

Illustrated by **Valeri Gorbachev**

Houghton Mifflin Company
Boston New York 1996

*Author's Note*

The story structure of *Young Mouse and Elephant* indicates that its origins lie in India, as Mouse's encounters with three creatures before finding Elephant follow a pattern found in Indian folktales. From India, the tale spread from country to country; a version of the story can be found in *Turkish Folktales for Children*, retold by Barbara K. Walker (Hamden, Conn.: Linnet Pub., 1988). The story also has elements of a basic folktale plot found in many countries, "Learning to Fear Man," in which man sets out to find "man," encountering different animals along his journey. Finally man meets "man," who promptly beats him, and thus man learns to fear man. This story was known and told among the Kanure-speaking group of the Bornu region, who lived in an area west of Lake Chad in the Sudan, the locale where this version of *Young Mouse and Elephant* was told.

9835043

Text copyright © 1996 by Pamela J. Farris
Illustrations copyright © 1996 by Valeri Gorbachev

All rights reserved. For information about permission to reproduce selections from this book, write to Permissions, Houghton Mifflin Company, 215 Park Avenue South, New York, New York 10003.

For information about this and other Houghton Mifflin trade and reference books and multimedia products, visit The Bookstore at Houghton Mifflin on the World Wide Web at (http://www.hmco.com/trade/).

Library of Congress Cataloging-in-Publication Data

Farris, Pamela J.
  Young Mouse and Elephant : an East African folktale / Pamela J. Farris : illustrated by Valeri Gorbachev.
       p.  cm.
  Summary: Young Mouse, sure he is the strongest animal on the African savannah, goes in search of the elephant, to "break it apart and stomp it to bits."
  ISBN 0-395-73977-2
  [1. Folklore—Africa.]   I. Gorbachev, Valeri, ill.   II. Title.
PZ8.1.F2235Yo   1996
398.2—dc20        94-48835   CIP   AC
[E]

Printed in Singapore.

TWP   10   9   8   7   6   5   4   3   2   1

*For Kurtis, my young mouse* —P.J.F.

*To my wife, Victoria, and to my children,
Sasha and Konstantin* —V.G.

In the lush grass of the savanna, there lived a village of mice. And in that village there was one mouse who was very strong and very proud. No mouse could throw farther or run faster or out-wrestle him.

One day Young Mouse was sitting by his grandfather's hut crushing dried grass in his paws.

"You know, Grandfather," said Young Mouse, "I'm very strong. Why, I'm the strongest mouse in the whole village."

"That's true," said Grandfather.

"Why, I'm so strong, I must be the strongest animal on the plains," Young Mouse declared.

Grandfather was old and wise. "You are indeed strong. But Elephant is the strongest animal on the plains. She might not like to hear you bragging."

"Elephant!" shouted Young Mouse. "Why, I can break Elephant apart and stomp her to bits, for I am the strongest animal on the plains!" And with that, Young Mouse marched off to find Elephant.

Grandfather smiled to himself. "Well, come back soon, Young Mouse, for a storm is coming," he called.

Young Mouse came upon a lizard basking in the last of the sun. Young Mouse marched right up. "Hey! Are you Elephant?"

"No, I'm just a lizard."

"In that case consider yourself fortunate," Young Mouse said, "for if you had been Elephant, I would have broken you apart and stomped you to bits."

The lizard gave a great sigh, for he had seen Elephant. When Young Mouse saw him, he stomped his paw on the ground.

Just at that moment came a roaring clap of thunder.

"The little mouse made the sky tremble!" cried the lizard, and he lumbered away to hide under a bush.

Satisfied, Young Mouse puffed out his chest and marched across the plains to seek out Elephant. He saw a zebra resting lazily. Young Mouse marched right up. "Hey! Are you Elephant?"

"No, I'm a zebra," came the reply.

"In that case consider yourself fortunate," said Young Mouse, "for if you had been Elephant, I would have broken you apart and stomped you to bits."

The zebra simply snorted for she knew Elephant. When the Young Mouse heard her, he glared. Just then a bolt of lightning flashed across the sky.

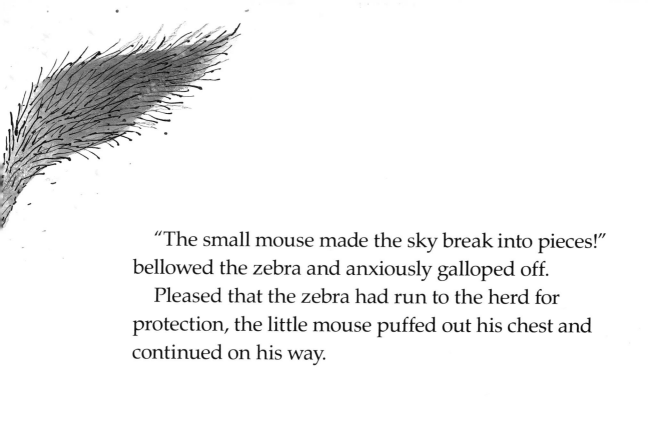

"The small mouse made the sky break into pieces!" bellowed the zebra and anxiously galloped off.

Pleased that the zebra had run to the herd for protection, the little mouse puffed out his chest and continued on his way.

He saw a giraffe busy nibbling leaves. Young Mouse marched right up. "Hey! Are you Elephant?"

The giraffe lowered his head.

"They call me a giraffe."

"In that case consider yourself fortunate," said the Young Mouse, "for if you had been Elephant, I would have broken you apart and stomped you to bits."

The giraffe merely shrugged and flicked his ears. When Young Mouse saw him, he shook his paw. At that moment, a large rain cloud darkened the entire sky.

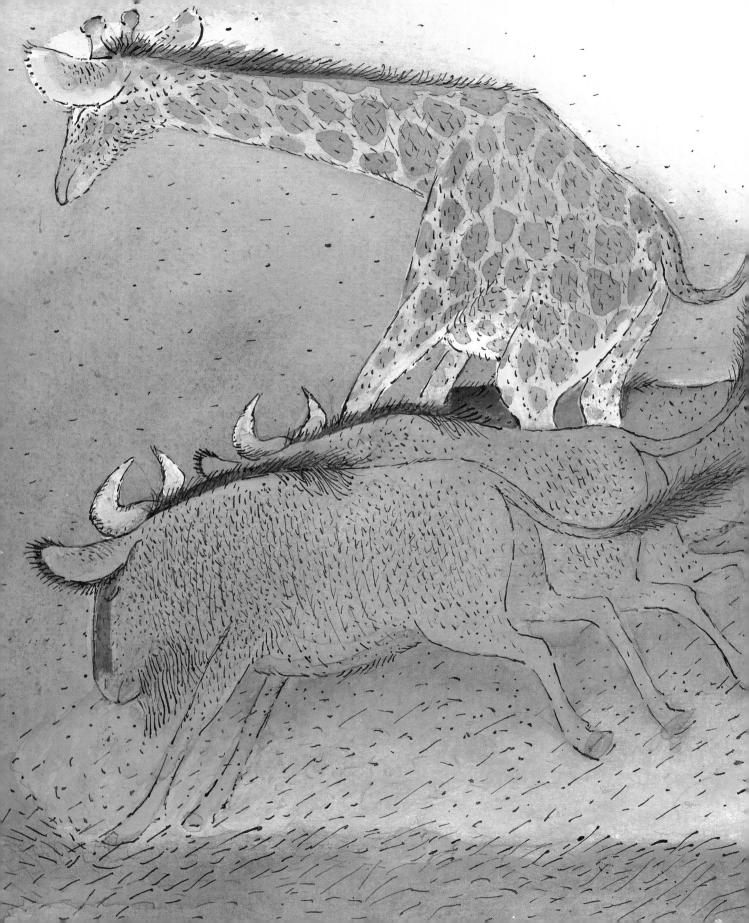

"The tiny mouse caused the sun to leave the sky!" shouted the giraffe as he raced off in fear.

The other animals saw the giraffe running and they started running too.

"They are all afraid of me," Young Mouse said and puffed out his chest even more.

Soon Young Mouse came upon an enormous animal with legs as big as tree trunks. It had two tails, a small one in back and a large one in front. It was the biggest animal he had ever seen. Young Mouse marched right up. "Hey! Are you Elephant?"

Elephant turned to see who was talking. She looked and looked but only saw trees, bushes, and rocks.

"Hey! Are you Elephant?" the voice repeated.

Elephant looked around once more. Squinting her eyes, she spotted a small speck. It was Young Mouse. Elephant leaned down to hear better.

"Are you Elephant?" yelled Young Mouse again.

"Yes, Elephant is my name."

Young Mouse puffed up his chest. "Well, I've been looking for you. I'm the strongest animal on the plains. Just what do you think of that?"

Elephant stood a moment, then she slowly filled her trunk with water. WHOOSH! A great flood of water hit Young Mouse. He tumbled head over heels across the savanna.

Soon rain began to fall, first in droplets and later much harder. When the storm had passed, Young Mouse woke up and looked around. Elephant was nowhere to be seen.

"Hump! The storm must have washed Elephant away," Young Mouse announced. "In that case Elephant should consider herself fortunate, for I would have broken her apart and stomped her to bits!"